The Proto-ocean for
Co-consciousness

圖錄
Plates

相信青年的無限可能
朝由共識形成的主題樂園邁進
台北當代藝術館館長／駱麗真

本館從 2021 年起推出的「青年策展人計畫」，鼓勵支持年輕策展工作者，以及剛踏入策展領域的策展人，能夠於專業正式的展覽平台，發表分享個人獨到的見解與專業。首屆「青年策展人計畫」邀請黃又文、馮馨與彼勇‧依斯瑪哈單等三位策展人，從現實社會、科技視角及原民力量討論出發，舉辦展覽「為了明天的進行式」，充滿創意及新世代的觀察，後續為展覽帶出多重極具意義的討論。今年，「青年策展人計畫」由策展人孫以臻的「共識覺」與王韓芳「主題樂園幻想工程挑戰賽」分別於館內一、二樓舉行。

孫以臻、王韓芳兩位策展人都具有科學學習的背景，孫以臻大學主修生物科學，後續轉往藝術策展領域，從她過往策劃的展覽可以看到許多跨領域結合科學思維與藝術表現的內容。本檔「共識覺」當中，策展人邀請六位／組國內外藝術創作者，從「人類的共識如何達成？」這個富含直覺的提問出發，拉出人類與非人類、人類與異世界當中，關於社會政治與科技發展等相互映照的關係。策展人王韓芳則從社會樂園化的面向切入，在「主題樂園幻想工程挑戰賽」將六位不同國家的藝術家比擬為迪士尼樂園當中的幻想工程師，在策展人所建構起的環境內，觀眾帶著既像勞動者又似表演者的多元身分，隨著動線穿梭在每件藝術作品及空間元素當中，逐步揭露這座去脈絡化的主題樂園所展現及形構的社會運行機制和方法，映照出一片有別日常的平行宇宙。

本檔展覽感謝許多贊助單位的共同支持：THERMOS 膳魔師、當代藝術基金會、財團法人紀慧能藝術文化基金會、老爺會館、台灣愛普生科技股份有限公司、台灣索尼股份有限公司、中央廣播電台、國立臺北藝術大學關渡美術館、臺北市立建成國中、台北電影節、Yogibo、奧地利聯邦總理府藝術文化、公共服務暨運動部（Federal Ministry for Arts, Culture, Civil Service and Sport, Republic of Austria）等單位，在諸方共識相互凝聚下，於本館順利創造出一座現實與虛構並存的主題樂園。

Believe in the Infinite Possibilities of Young Talents —
Towards the Theme Park Formed by Co-consciousness

Director of MoCA TAIPEI / Li-Chen Loh

Since 2021, MoCA TAIPEI initiated the Emerging Curator Program to encourage emerging curators to present their insights and profession through a professional exhibition platform. In the first year of the Emerging Curator Program, MoCA TAIPEI invited three curators—Erica Yu-Wen Huang, Feng Hsin and Biung Ismahasan to present the exhibition *Tomorrow, Towarding*, tackling issues from different angles, ranging from realistic society and technology to indigenous power. With innovative and new generation perspectives, the exhibition generates meaningful and multifaceted discussions. For this year, the curators of MoCA's 2022 Emerging Curator Program—Yi-Cheng Sun and Wang Han-Fang, bring us the exhibitions *The Proto-ocean for Co-consciousness* and *Making Worlds: An Imagineering Project*, which were held at MoCA's exhibition galleries respectively at first floor and second floor.

Yi-Cheng Sun and Wang Han-Fang are both with background of learning science. Yi-Cheng Sun majored in Life Science and later turned to curating. From past exhibitions she has curated, we could see many works with cross-disciplinary content combining science and art. In the exhibition *The Proto-ocean for Co-consciousness*, the curator invites 6 artists/ artist collectives and begins with the instinctive question— "How do we bring about the co-consciousness?" underlining the relationships between the social political and scientific development in the human/ nonhuman, human/heterogeneous world. The curator Wang Han-Fang explores the Disneyfication of the society and pictures 6 participating artists as imagineers of the theme park. In the environment built by the curator, members of the audience are like laborers and performers; they follow the designated traffic flow and pass through each artwork and spacial element, and gradually disclose the mechanisms and methods that the decontextualized theme park has presented and formed.

The exhibitions are made possible thanks to our sponsors: THERMOS; Contemporary Art Foundation; Ji Huei-Neng Art and Culture Foundation; Royal Inn, Epson Taiwan; SONY; Radio Taiwan International; Kuandu Museum of Fine Arts, Taipei National University of the Arts; Jian Cheng Junior High School; Taipei Film Festival; Yogibo; Federal Ministry for Arts, Culture, Civil Service and Sport, Republic of Austria, and more. By forming co-consciousness with multiple people involved, MoCA TAIPEI has successfully created a "theme park" in which reality and imagination coexist.

策展論述／專文 Curatorial Statement／Essay

展覽「共識覺」的概念發想自 2021 年的台灣。在疫情最緊張的那一年，往日生活中的會議、教學、共食和小酌時光，從辦公大樓、學校教室、餐廳、酒吧紛紛轉換到 Zoom、Google Meet、Gather Town 和更多不同的線上場域。歷經這段變化的過程中特別觸動筆者的是，當國家和城市的邊界近乎封閉，人們卻總能重新找到不同的方式連結彼此。當溝通的媒介改變，共感和連結方式也隨之改變——也許是一場讓萬人以數位替身齊聚的線上演唱會，也許是一個或笑或哭的表情符號，也或許，是透過一種更加幽微的信息交換方式——都令我們仍舊能夠感覺自己與他者同在。在全球疫這場劇烈的變化中，被強行封閉的門就像一面鏡反射出另一扇門，引領著本展試探更多種穿越時空與物質基礎，但仍舊使得意識同在得以可能。特別是在美術館的場域中，本展試探著以藝術創作打開一個又一個全新的意識場域。

從英文的語意理解，consciousness（意識）是由「con：一起、聚合」加上「sci：知道」與「ous：很多」所組成，而在中文的語意中，「意識」有著「對世界的感覺、思維等各種心理過程之總和」的意涵。本展在這樣的意涵之上進行意義的擴充，展名「共識覺」可以理解為在兩個以上的意識體生成，且同在或互相滲透之後，不同於以單一個體為主，所能夠經驗與知道的能力。這樣的能力或者經驗可能因為長期被忽略而失去，因此也可以視為是一種等待被啟動的本能。當今，這樣的能力與經驗雖曖昧未明，卻同時在人類文明與技術的發展中呼之欲出。

2022 年，美國奇幻電影《媽的多重宇宙》以共時並進的多重宇宙觀，拿下全球破億的亮眼票房成績。劇中的女主角秀蓮（楊紫瓊飾演）以「宇宙搖」（Verse Jumping），和平行宇宙中命運迥異的自己及家人相遇後和解。穿梭在多重宇宙的冒險中，共時與同在成為破解單一敘事觀點中宿命論的解方。而諾貝爾獎委員會則像是不約而同地，將該年度的物理獎項頒發給研究「量子糾纏」理論的三位科學家，Alain Aspect、John F. Clauser 以及 Anton Zeilinger，昭示著前驅的科學研究社群對「糾纏態」的理解，又向前邁進了一大步。以白話的方式來理解，量子糾纏的重大發現在於認識到一對處於糾纏態的粒子，即便彼此相距甚遠，也會時時刻刻以超越光速的方式互相影響。從全球電影票房排行榜到科學研究的最高殿堂，常民社會與專業知識社群的發展似乎都鼓舞著自詡以藝術來認識及創造世界的藝文工作者，勇敢地跳脫既有認知中對於時空、肉身、語言乃至身為人的種種限制，透過藝術實踐重新理解意識的生成及存在。

回溯科學家一般認為生物圈最早的意識，衪來自地球的原始海洋。這片凝結了大氣中的水氣才得以聚集的水體，不只改變了生命誕生之前，地球上空氣的組成與整體的自然環境，更重要的是，它保護和滋養了最早的意識誕生。我們也可以說，有了原始海洋，才讓這一切成真。然而，當時間飛逝地運轉了數十億年，當今人類的生活、生存與生命狀態，都隨著科技的發展、環境的變遷、疫情的籠罩，甚至典型與非典型戰爭的爆發，處於一種過渡與轉換階段，若我們期待一種新的意識體誕生，以此作為找到身為人，重新認識自身與他者關係的方法。藝術創作有可能如同聚集的水體，成為那片滋養與保護新意識體誕生的原始海洋嗎？在本展中，對於共同意識體如何誕生的假設，將建立在一種更加仰賴互動技術與資訊交換的基礎上，並主張以此作為「共識」得以誕生的條件。

對筆者而言當代藝術的創作者的獨特之處，不只在於勇於嘗試以技術作為創作媒介，更在於以技術的政治作為關注對象的企圖心。因此若以此對共同意識中的技術展開拆解、重建與探究，將使得在這片原始海洋裡誕生的，不僅是一種新的意識狀態，或覺知他者意識的能力，過程中反覆照出的更是關乎當代社會中的技術、政治與共同體的寓言空間。

在展覽的入口形象展區，來自藝術家雙人組好奇機 CURIOSKI（李懿澐＆鄭伊婷）的作品《意識景觀系列》，視 VR 裝置為作品情境中的「人腦外掛」，邀請觀眾透過「外掛」在虛擬實境中展開意識與肉身、與資訊、與自我的探索。而作品所在的展區兩側，大面的鏡像中有著無限生成的虛空間，意象上回應的是虛擬實境作為一種新興的技術以及創作媒介，為美術館觀眾帶來虛實交雜的新體驗場域。此外，也以此作為本展對共同意識互相映照、生成的想像。

105 展間中，來自黃鼎云的創作計畫《神的棲所 GiR》在經過長期的田野調查後，提出作品《空耳乩》與演員廖原慶展開一場「飾演乩童起乩」的排演練習；作品《化景練習》則邀請觀眾在聲光引導中展開「與神同在」的練習。潛身在台灣的文化脈絡與宗教信仰中，《神的棲所 GiR》透過藝術創作中的靈活調度，試圖再現、解構與技術化的是人與神同在一具肉身之中的意識狀態。

位在前後展區交界處蓋伊・班・阿里的作品《cellF》，借助組織培養等技術在體外培養來自藝術家自身的神經細胞網絡，並視之為自己的「外部大腦」。蓋伊・班・阿里以異於慣常的方式使用技術，並且在藝術的語境中不斷創造生物學意義上不存在的象徵性的「外腦」，以此與各國的音樂家展開即興聲響演出。無時不引誘著觀者在科學知識、技術和象徵意義中揣想，從藝術家的身體外延而生的「外腦」，以及他／她可能發展出的智慧或創造性潛能。

正當諸多的電影、文學作品與懷疑論者擔憂著，人工智慧有一日終將生成自我意識，並且以一種超越人類能夠掌握的姿態，反噬他的創造者。在 106 展間，胥貝拉・佩區克的作品《PL'AI》視無規則也非競爭性的「遊戲」為所有生命體的本體狀態，並以此作為編寫、創造人工智慧的原始意圖，旨在探索植物與人工智慧的共生與同在。植株的生長將如何與人工的智慧相互形塑呢？未知的生長與互動，巧妙地將我們從人類中心的思維，轉向對於非人物種、無生命的他者及其意識狀態的思索。

107 展間，動態自造實驗室的 VR 作品《Project ZERO｜首部曲》從傳奇舞者蕭賀文生命的頓然消逝，望向留存於世的大量數位檔案。創作團隊嘗試著延續有限生命在數位時空中留下的痕跡——他們掃描並重建逝者生命中的重要場景、捕捉並運算無數排演紀錄中逝者的身體動態資料——探究的是面對逝去的生命，新興數位技術在意識的延續可能扮演的角色為何？以及藉此創造生者與死者同在於虛擬實境中的可能。

展場中的最後一件作品，lololol（林亭君＆張欣）從幾乎成為所有科技物基礎的「半導體」出發，探索在人與科技物之間流轉的能量及其韻律。在作品《晶舟靈雨》中，包覆性的視覺、聽覺、觸覺與震動覺，乃至全黑的展間，都像是邀請著每一位走進作品的觀眾，以最直接的身體感受去想像一個自身與半導體晶格網同在的意識場域。穿插在晶格的影像之間，熟悉的街景和 101 辦公大樓上一路向天際延伸而去的窗格，則帶著我們的身體與意識回到每日生活在台北，以及那個「矽島」台灣坐落其中的全球技術產業生產鏈。

就如同占星術、自然科學、大數據或演算法等知識系統或技術——無論身處當代的你相信與否——它們的出現都（曾）提供了人們一套將自己與整個宇宙、自然或人類社會連為一體的認識方法。為了探索與拓展最大幅員的共識狀態與覺知經驗，以此作為在巨變的時代中找到身為人，重新認識自身與他者關係的方法，「共識覺」的展出作品廣泛涉及了「意識與肉身」、「生者與亡者」、「人類與神靈」、「非人物種與資訊體」乃至「人類社會與科技物」。這樣一個對共同意識進行探索的展覽，在議題的選擇上看似虛幻，甚至給人一種缺乏物質基礎或者身體經驗置喙的印象，但事實上，展覽作為一種面向公眾的藝術實踐，本展更加仰賴的是來訪的觀眾以一種「接觸即興」的方式與作品相遇。因為當智性的知識未及，而身體經驗又仍在形成當中，坐落在理解與困惑的接觸地帶，觀眾唯一（或僅剩）能夠仰賴的便是以極度主觀的經驗，展開屬於他／她與作品之間獨有的共識場域。此外本展亦期許，在當代藝術慣常的自反性中，能引發來訪的觀眾產生一種不斷回頭檢視場域中的技術組成，與其政治性的自主遞迴的姿態。

The Proto-ocean for Co-consciousness

The Proto-ocean for Co-consciousness was inspired by the everyday life of Taiwan in 2021, which was the peak of the pandemic. As a result, places for meetings, teaching, dining together, and drinking shifted from offices, classrooms, restaurants, and bars to Zoom, Google Meet, Gather Town, and other online platforms. I was particularly impressed by how people can always find different ways to connect during this period of transformation when the borders and cities are closed. When the medium of communication changes, so do the way of empathy and connection—be it an online concert where thousands of people gather as digital avatars, a laughing or crying emoji, or a more subtle way of exchanging information—but we can still sense that we are in the company of the others. In this severe disturbance of the global pandemic, the forcibly closed gateway is like a mirror reflecting another door. It leads this exhibition to explore more possibilities to travel through time, space, and material basis with consciousness retained. This exhibition particularly attempts to open up new fields of consciousness through artistic creations.

Semantically, the English word "consciousness" is composed of "con" ("together" or "to aggregate") and the combination of "sci" ("know") and "ous" ("many"). In Chinese, "Yi-shih" means "the sum of various mental processes such as feeling and thinking for the world." *The Proto-ocean for Co-consciousness* builds upon and aims to expand these meanings. Its title can be understood as the formation, coexistence, or inter-permeation of two or more consciousness, resulting in a perceptive ability and experience – which might have been lost under long-term neglect; so, it can also be regarded as an innate ability waiting to be awakened – different from an individual's. Today, although such abilities and experiences remain hazy, they gradually emerge from human civilization and technological development.

In 2022, the American Sci-fi fantasy *Everything Everywhere All at Once* became a blockbuster hit with its synchronized multiverse, with a thriving global box office of over 100 million. The heroine, Evelyn Quan Wang (played by Michelle Yeoh), encounters and reconciles with herself and her family members with different fates in the parallel universe through "Verse Jumping." In the adventurous multiple universes traveling, simultaneity and coexistence become the solution to overcome fatalism from a single narrative point of view. Coincidentally, the Nobel Prize Committee awarded the Nobel Prize in Physics 2022 to three scientists researching the theory of "quantum entanglement," Alain Aspect, John F. Clauser, and Anton Zeilinger, attesting that the leading scientific community's understanding of "entangled state" has taken another big step forward. In plain words, the significant discovery of quantum entanglement is the realization that what happens to one of the particles in an entangled pair determines what happens to the other particle with a speed faster than the speed of light, even if they are far apart. From the global blockbuster to the highest scientific honor, the development of civil society and professional fields seem to encourage creators who claim to understand and create the world through art to think out of the box bravely and break away from the limitations of time and space, physical body, language, and human beings to shed new lights on the understanding of generation and existence of consciousness through artistic practice.

Scientists generally believe that the earliest consciousness of the biosphere came from the proto-ocean of Earth. This water body, which accumulated and condensed from the water vapor in the atmosphere, not only changed the composition of the air and the overall natural environment on Earth before the birth of life but, more importantly, protected and nourished the earliest-born consciousness. We can also say consciousness could not come into being without the proto-ocean. However, as billions of years fly by, the living condition, existence, and state of life of human beings today are in a transitional phase under technological developments, environmental changes, global pandemics, and the outbreak of conventional and unconventional wars. Suppose we expect the birth of a new consciousness as a way to find ourselves as human beings and understand the relationship between ourselves and others anew. Can artworks converge into a water body, a primitive ocean that nourishes and protects the birth of a new consciousness? In this exhibition, the hypothesis of how the co-consciousness is born will be based on a foundation that relies more on interactive technology and information exchange and advocates this as the condition for the birth of "co-consciousness" or even "consensus."

I believe the uniqueness of contemporary artists lies not only in their courage to deploy new technology as media but also in their ambition to focus on the politics of technology. Therefore, if we disassemble, reconstruct, and explore the technologies in the co-consciousness from this perspective, what will be born out of this proto-ocean is not only a new state of consciousness or the ability to perceive the consciousness of others. Instead, the process constantly stimulates reflections and creates an allegorical space related to technologies, politics, and communities in contemporary society.

A Glimpse of the Mind Landscapes by CURIOSKI (Yi-Ho Li & Yi-Ting Cheng) occupies the entrance hall. The artist duo regard the VR device as an "external human brain" in the context of the work and invite the audience to use the "plug-in" to launch an exploration of consciousness and body, information, and self in the VR universes. Large-scale mirrors on both sides of the entrance hall generate an infinite virtual space, an imagery that responds to the fact that VR – an emerging technology and art medium – brings a new experience field of mixed virtual and tangible to the audience. In addition, it also serves as this exhibition's echoing imagination of mutual reflection and generation of co-consciousness.

God in Residency, Ding-Yun Huang's project in Room 105, is a brainchild based on long-term fieldwork. In *Misheard Medium*, actor Yuan-Ching Liao participates in a rehearsal exercise of "acting a medium being possessed by a deity." On the other hand, *Scenario Incarnation* invites the audience to practice "being with God" under the guidance of sound and light. Embedded in Taiwan's cultural context and religious beliefs, *God in Residency* attempts to represent, deconstruct, and technicalize the state of consciousness in which humans and God are in the same body through flexible deployment in artistic creation.

Located at the central stairway is Guy Ben-Ary's *cellF*, which adopts techniques such as tissue culture to cultivate the artist's nerve cell network in vitro – the artist regards it as his "external brain." Guy Ben-Ary uses technology in an unusual way and creates a symbolic "external brain" in the context of art. He continues to make a symbolic "external brain" that does not exist biologically to improvise sound performances with musicians worldwide. *cellF* had an enduring power to attract viewers to speculate scientifically, technologically, and symbolically that the "external brain" extends from the artist's body and the wisdom or creative potential they might develop.

Many movies, literary works, and skeptics are worried that AI will one day generate self-awareness and – in a manner beyond human control – turn around to destroy its creator. However, Špela Petrič's *PL'AI* in Room 106 regards the "game" without rules and non-competition as the ontological state of all living organisms. Petrič plays with this idea as the original intention of populating and creating AI, aiming to explore the symbiosis and coexistence relationship between plants and AI. How can the growth of plants and AI affect each other? Focusing on the development and interaction of the unknown, this work subtly shifts us from anthropocentric thinking to ponder over non-human species, lifeless others, and their states of consciousness.

In Room 107, FabLab Dynamic's VR work *Project ZERO | Episode One* is inspired by the dearly departed legendary dancer Hsiao Ho-Wen and utilizes the large number of digital documents she left for the world. The team tries to expand the traces left by limited life in digital space – scanning and reconstructing essential scenes in the life of the dancer, capturing and calculating the dynamic data of the dancer in

與缺席共同思考

展覽「共識覺」由策展人孫以臻策劃，涉及「意識」此一龐大主題。其中，有些事物不見了，或者說，我們不記得有些事物不見了。

「影像是缺席的再現，當然有些事物不見了！」或許有些人會這麼說。

不過，真正不在場的並非古典意義上的指涉對象——既不是藝術本身，也不是影像中的人物或物體。在這些不在場的背後，有些微弱的事物拒絕被概括在那樣的概念之下——這引起了我的關注。我認為此展覽所展出的一些作品中所蘊含的神秘不在場，具備在原始海洋的底部為「共識覺」形成一種凝聚力、一個空隙的可能。

「零」是不在場的抽象雙胞胎，我想由此談起。約公元前三世紀，零首次出現在瑪雅曆法；在此之前，零在計算動物、財產或時間等日常活動中沒有任何地位。經驗豐富的埃及數學家也沒有在幾何學與占星術中發現零的概念。巴比倫人試圖區分數字 1 與 60 [1] 的表示方式時發明了零，並且以由左至右的符號表示帶分數。他們的做法是以兩個傾斜的楔形文字來表示算盤上的空格或空列，而這種「佔位」符號賦予巴比倫數列獨特的意義。人類學家泰倫斯·狄肯（Terrence Deacon）認為其特性是本質上的不存在性。[2] 就「零」的意義而言，不在場是永遠存在的「不存在的東西」，因為其存在源自於它的不在場本質。這種不在場現象滲透、組織我們經驗中的物質領域，是沒有物質對應的潛能——除了引發實質後果或具體行動。我忝用狄肯的概念，透過書寫此展中的作品來探索我所關注的「不在場」。

人如何思索不在場？首先，我要進行告解：以藝術在物質世界中具有特定尺寸、重量、紋理等物理屬性作為考量，本展的兩件生物藝術作品 [3]——蓋伊·班·阿里的《cellF》與胥貝拉·佩區克的《PL'AI》促使我徘徊思索「不存在」之議題。

這兩件作品以錄像紀錄與藝術家敘述呈現。[4] 我們馬上可以注意到直接的不在場——這些生物藝術作品位於展間之外，某個不在台灣的地方。它們服膺於藝術家的想像力，並且藉由紀錄片來傳達藝術家的想法及訊息。觀眾當然可以就此打住——看完錄像，留下無限驚嘆，腦中資訊超載。這看似全知的位置隱含著一種慾望，期待現實能夠在知識、技術以及（無可避免的）權力所緊密構成的場域中被加以審查與分析——評斷便隨之而來，至少是以學科知識的名義，導致作品的審美價值受到威脅。那個位置假設這些紀錄片是已知的事實、是理所當然的。我們可以說在科學及專業看法能夠支持藝術的教育價值之同時，我們也不能排拒在知識進入之前，第一次觀看紀錄片時所經驗的任何感受。那是一種我們在日常生活中不完全熟悉、還無法習慣的世界所獨具的感覺，無論是由什麼事物所觸發的都有其目的。激發某種感覺的動力暗示了一系列由外部關係所賦予特徵的結果：呈現這些生物藝術作品的紀錄片體現了作品所不是的樣態的想像。由於某些物質及非物質的限制，作品無法以實物呈現。這些限制的不在場性推動了創作流程，使每部紀錄片在時空中成為此時此刻的樣態——紀錄片並非一種用來填補由「是」或「應該」所支持的物質性或理想性的空缺。就此而言，每件作品之所以能成為作品以及如何運作或呈現，都是在不同情況下受到「不存在的存在」所限制的結果。

countless rehearsal records – they explore the role that emerging digital technologies may play in the continuation of consciousness as we encounter the passing of life. They also create the possibility that the living and the dead meet in VR.

The last work in the exhibition is created by lololol (Xia Lin & Sheryl Cheung). Based on "semiconductor" – it has almost become the basis of all technological objects – it explores the energy and rhythm that flow between people and technological objects. With enveloping visual, auditory, tactile, and vibratory sensations in the pitch-black room, *Wafer Bearer Deep Rain* seems to invite every audience who walks into the space to experience it with the most direct physical senses and to imagine a field of consciousness in which they are with the semiconductor lattice. Interspersed between the images of the lattice are familiar streets and the panes of Taipei 101 stretching up to the sky, leading our body and consciousness back to our daily life in Taipei and the global technology industry production chain where Taiwan, the "Silicon Island," locates in.

Astrology, natural science, big data, and algorithm – whether one living in the contemporary era believes in them or not – the appearance of these knowledge systems or technics provides/provided people with a set of epistemological skills to connect themselves with the entire cosmos, nature, or human society. Therefore, to explore and expand the state of co-consciousness and perceptive experiences to the widest, the artworks featured in this exhibition involve an extensive range of topics, including "consciousness and corporeality," "the living and the dead," "human beings and divine existences," "non-human species and information," and "human society and technical artifacts." Such an exhibition that probes into co-consciousness seems illusory in the choice of topics and even gives people the impression that it is being judgemental without material foundation or bodily experience. In fact, as an art practice facing the public, this exhibition depends more on the audience encountering the works through "contact and improvisation."

Because when intellectual knowledge is not yet prevailed, and bodily experience is still being formed, situated in the contact zone of understanding and confusion, the only thing (or the only thing left) that the audience can rely on is their own highly subjective experience to unfold the unique co-consciousness field with the artworks. In addition, this exhibition also wishes that, in the customary reflexivity of contemporary art, it can trigger the audience to constantly reflect on the field's technical composition and its political self-return.

文／陳安捷

換句話說，不在場性沒有物質上的對應，而只是以概念體現於物質集合之中。

以《cellF》為例，這樣的想法意味著它作為藝術不僅僅是體外神經網絡、一個單一的結果、一個奇觀。它不只是透過知識（權力）的技術（實踐）在人工與自然二元論中建立的分類學的空白[5] 所展演出的可能性。在《cellF》創作之前及之外，存在多組單一性的限制條件，其中發生的一系列事件產生了未必符合作品最終目的形式。從這些限制所催生的事件中湧現的形式至少包括：濕實驗室培養幹細胞的特定配置、決定神經網絡規模的麥芽瓊脂培養皿、為神經網絡反應所訂製的合成器組件、每一場表演的空間，材料與技術編排以及紀錄片。如此一來，「具象」意味著藝術透過這些形式揭示了局限性。即《cellF》作為一個形式的集合，不是幹細胞或神經網絡內部運作的單一解釋，因此具有一種向四面八方流動、轉瞬即逝的物質性，尚待人們在其當前狀態之外進行探索。

本文至此已經看起來不太合理了，而我明白自己以這種方式書寫不在場，可能冒著極大的風險。我的意圖是在展覽中那些可能來得太快，去得太急的審美經驗裡或是於本展作品的表象中對抗在面對事物時的熟悉感。無論堅持不存在的因素看似多麼沒有意義又不必要，藝術家在《PL'AI》中維持對自我的批判，呈現出的並不只是一種自作聰明、看似「非人類」概念化的小黃瓜植株，還展現出藝術家反人類中心主義的慾望，並且提醒著人們古典再現的不足。[6] 此作透過嬉戲，或阿多諾所謂的「嬉戲元素」，[7] 一種「透過遊戲，而非理性」[8] 關注審美的藝術策略，以受不存在性所驅動的創作過程來處理小黃瓜植株及其與人工智慧所產生的各種變化。在有些乏味、由限制佔據主導地位而顯得平庸的生長條件下，我們注意到自己對在小黃瓜植株與人工智慧之間的相互作用知之甚少，而這正是作品的寶貴之處。藝術作為一系列涉及小黃瓜植株內、外部的奇特行為，使其變得陌生——它不再是我們所熟知的小黃瓜。同樣地，我們也無法想像或是預測這個與小黃瓜互動的人工智慧的未來。為了假裝面向未來而為藝術「指定」任何意義是令人欣慰但無效的，因為藝術「不是積極的、立即出現的」，[9] 一旦加諸這種意圖，藝術行動便會消解。《PL'AI》奠基於即時數據，其意圖相當明確：透過一種異化當下的手法，擾動科學探究中已知與未知的界限，探索邁向某種未來政治的一個可能。

藝術能夠透過強調不在場，使大量關於生命的事物浮現出來——確切地說，是生命為何——以及人類如何與超出我們當前智性所能理解的事物產生連結。不存在性指出在目前尚未為某種目的完全概念化的邊緣現實中，物質可能與何相關，故造成這種物質的非同一性。[10] 因此，它打開了一個裂縫，能夠通往曾經被拒絕的可能性。物質不再為了服務我們而存在，不為人類生活增添意義，不被物化為單一身分、[11] 風格、關係、信仰的構建或延續，不為保護或改善人類生活的現狀。事實上，當我們在生活中否認物質的真實性時，與這樣的存在之間的距離卻出奇地接近——因為我們繼續選擇活在危機感的另一面。為了對抗台灣獨有的危機，藝術雙人組 lololol（林亭君 & 張欣）的作品《晶舟靈雨》以口吃回應。正如作品標題所暗示，一張微晶片圖像所包含的不僅是搖擺的國家身分或地緣政治利益，還涵蓋了環境及勞動力剝削的議題。換句話說，半導體產業被神化，並且被人們以關於經濟成長、政治與生態危機的混合語言讚揚——加上驕傲、恐懼、憤怒、無能為力等複雜情緒，它成為一團巨大的糾纏物質，為了構建單一身分被同時賦予神話與悲劇的意義。那些看似扭曲而模糊不清、虛幻又深不可測的錄像藝術出自真實的景觀——彰顯產業（一種理想）的事物——以及變化，同時構成島嶼（一個實在的主體）。作品渺無定形而引人入勝，在危機二元化 [12] 的概念下，重現台灣半導體產業受到強大概念化的破壞所掩蓋的意志。觀者會發現自己直接面對不存在性、非同一性的微晶片、半導體產業以及（如果願意承認的話）台灣。作品中的每一張圖像都如口吃般期期艾艾，試圖與我們感官的另一面進行交流。也許口吃是一種語言，是它們的語言，也是我們的語言。開始探索我們感官的另一面——以及所有方面——我們就會開始口吃了。在結巴的話語中，物質不會從其無可馴服的本質發問：「你看到我了嗎？」而是主動邀請我們對於其不在場進行好奇的思考。

1 巴比倫數字系統為六十進位制，在 0 的表示法出現之前，數字 1 與 60 都採用同一個楔形文字表示。欲知零的歷史，請參閱查爾斯‧塞費（Charles Seife）的著作《零》（Zero）。

2 根據狄肯的說法，「不存在性」一詞用來「解釋產生生理與心理現象之過程的湧現與動態特性，而非不在場主義的形而上典範。」它是「矛盾的內在屬性，與缺失的、獨立的、可能不存在的事物有關。」（狄肯，《不完整的本質》，頁 577）

3 生物藝術是一種涉及生物學、細胞、濕組織或部分活體有機體的藝術實踐，藉由科學或偽科學實驗步驟來進行創作。

4 隨著電視節目──紀實影像結合涉入其中的人員的敘述──的發展並且在西方大眾媒體播出，這種視覺策略在藝術與展覽製作中蔚為風潮。這種節目所紀錄的真實，可以是重現過去事件的虛構或劇本演出，比如：重大刑事案件的實境秀或調查紀錄片。貝托爾特‧布萊希特（Bertolt Brecht）曾如此評論數位產出的圖像：「現在的情況變得極為複雜，導致現實的簡單再製所能告訴我們的內容都比過去來的少。」

5 根據藝術家的說法，體外神經網絡既不是人工智慧也不是自然智慧，因此它存在於「分類學的空白」，切勿與存在於任何基於知識的二元論之外的「不存在的空虛」相互混淆。

6 「……物體發揮概念時一定會留下提示，展現其違背傳統適當性的規範。」（阿多諾，《否定辯證法》，頁 5）

7 同上，頁 14。

8 同上。

9 同上，頁 15，頁 189。

10 在阿多諾對概念及其唯物主義的批判中，他認為所有概念的真理「指涉的是非概念性，因為概念本身是現實需要成形的時刻，其目的主要是為了控制自然，」而「改變概念性的方向，使其轉向非同一性，是否定辯證法的關鍵。」（阿多諾，《否定辯證法》，頁 11、12）

11 單一身分可以指個人身分、國家身分，或透過同化與認同所形成，壓抑差異及多樣性的集體身分。

12 不難看出在台灣的主流公共話語中，危機是深陷於國家認同建構之中的概念 - 現實。在這樣的論述之中，關於危機的不在場、危機裡的不在場以及危機本身的不在場，被定調、概念化、取代、掩蓋為某種特點，例如，在新冠危機中台灣在世界衛生組織的不在場被定義為「Taiwan Can Help」的口號，透過一系列的政治與物質操演來陳述與實現。

Thinking *with* Absences

The Proto-ocean for Co-consciousness (curated by Yi-Cheng Sun) engages with the great subject of consciousness. Some-things are missing, or some-things-missing are missing within.

"An image is the representation of an absence, of course there will be something missing!" some might say.

What exactly is missing, however, isn't the referent in a classical sense – not the art themselves nor the persons or objects in pictures. Behind those absences, however, something faint resists containment in that statement – it demands my attention. I consider the possibility of such enigmatic absences in the works forming a sort of cohesive gravity, a void, at the bottom of *the proto-ocean* for co-consciousness.

A twin of absence in abstract form, zero is the point where I'd like to start from. Before its first appearance in the Mayan calendar in around the 3rd century B.C., zero had no place in everyday activities – be it counting animals or possessions or passing time. Nor did the sophisticated Egyptian mathematicians discover the concept of zero in their geometry and astrology. Zero was born out of a problem of representation for the Babylonians when they tried to distinguish the number of 1 from that of 60[1] and denote mixed numbers via symbols from left to right. The solution was to use two slanted wedges to represent an empty space or an empty column on the abacus. This *placeholder* gives any of the Babylonian number sequence a unique meaning. Terrence Deacon considers this quality fundamentally *absential*.[2] Absence, in this sense of zero, is "something-not-there" *always* being there, owing its existence to its essential absence. Such absential phenomena infiltrate and organise the material realms of our experiences as potentiality without material correspondences – except when causing physical consequences or acts. I humbly borrow his concept in exploring the absence that preoccupies me through writing about the various works in this exhibition.

How might one think *with* such absence? To begin with, a confession first to be made: taking a work of art which has specific physical properties in the material world such as dimensions, weights, and textures, the two bio artworks[3] in the show – *cellF* by Guy Ben-Ary and *PL'AI* by Špela Petrič – are what made me wander to the question of the *absential*.

The works are represented by video documentations and narrations by the artists.[4] It takes little effort to notice the immediate absences – the bio artworks located somewhere outside of the gallery space, away from Taiwan. The artworks serve the artists' imaginations and are having their expressions or messages transmitted via documentaries. One could have stopped right there; finishing watching the videos, leaving awestruck and overloaded with information. At the core of this seemingly omniscient position is a desire to make reality reviewable and analysable for a densely constituted field of knowledge, techniques and inevitably, power – judgement could follow, in the names of disciplinary knowledge at least, leaving the aesthetic value of the artworks at risk. In that position is the assumption that the videos are something

By Theo Ussay

given, granted. Whilst scientific and disciplinary judgements could sustain, arguably, the value of art for educational functions, we cannot deny *any* feeling when watching the documentaries for the first time before knowledge comes in. It's a feeling specific to a world(s) that we are not at all familiar with, not yet capable of being used to, in our everyday life. Whatever initiates this feeling serves a purpose. A dynamic that prompts a feeling implies a chain of results characterised by an extrinsic relationship: the documentaries accounting for the bio artworks that embody the imaginations about something that these *are not*. The artworks cannot be physically present due to certain material and immaterial constraints. These constraints are absential, yet they drove the work processes that brought each of the documentaries to be *what-it-is* to this moment in time and space – a documentary is *not* a given to fulfil a physical or ideal void sustained by what something "is" or "should" be. In this sense, each artworks' ability to be what they are and how they operate or being represented is defined by constraints – by absential existences – in different specific circumstances, i.e., the absential has no material correspondences, but only to be embodied, as concepts, in assemblages of matter.

In the case of *cellF*, such thinking implies that it is not only the in-vitro neural network instrument, as a single outcome, a spectacle, that is the art. It is *not* only a performed possibility of a taxonomic void[5] that is established within a dualism of artificial and natural identified through techniques (practices) of knowledges (power). Prior to and *outside* of *cellF*, there were singular sets of conditions of constraints within which forms emerged from a series of events that took place that do not necessarily comply with the end purpose of *the* work. These forms include at least the specific setting of a wet lab for growing the stem cells, the MEA dish that defines the scale of the neural network, the components of the tailored synthesisers through which the neural network reacts, the spatial, material and technical arrangements of every performance taken place and the documentary. To be "representational" in this sense would mean that art *reveals* the concept of limitations via these embodiments, that *cellF*, as an *assemblage* of forms, is *not* an explanation of the internal process of the stem cells nor the neural network and therefore possesses a fleeting materiality that flows in all directions that is yet to be explored outside of its current being.

Already, something does not quite make sense and I am aware that I might be risking a lot in writing about absences in such terms. My intention is to antagonise the familiar when confronted by matter on the surface of the art or within the aesthetic experience that could come an end too fast in this show. However meaningless and unnecessarily it seems to stick with the absential causes, something prevails in *PL'AI* – a self-criticism demonstrating an anti-anthropocentric desire on the part of the artist – that does not pretend a clever, seemingly "non-human" conceptualisation of the cucumber plant, is a reminder of the inadequacy of classical representation.[6] The playfulness, or the "playful element" in Adorno's terms[7] is an artistic tactic for an attentive aesthetic "by play, not by reason"[8] through accessing the absential-driven work process of the cucumber plant and its various becomings with an AI. We are aware of that *little is known* from the interaction between the cucumber plant and the

AI in the condition that they grow – somehow dull, constraints reign in banality – this *is* the preciousness of the work. The art, as curious action in a series of encounters that takes into consideration of its inside and outside, defamiliarizes the cucumber plant – it is *not* the cucumber plant that we know of. Likewise, the AI is *not* what we can imagine or foresee. It is comfortably negating to "assign" any meaning for ostensible future-orientated purposes to the art for art, being "not positively and immediately at hand",[9] dissolves through such action. Grounded in real-time data, *PL'AI* has a clear intention: to trouble the boundaries between knowing and unknowing in scientific inquiry through a present process of estrangement for exploring the possibilities towards a kind of politics yet-to-come.

By foregrounding absences, art can bring to the surface an overwhelming number of things concerning life – what a life *is* to be precise – and how humans relate to it beyond the comprehensible sphere of our current intellect. The *absential* pointing to what a matter *might be about* in a border reality *in present* that is not fully conceptualised for any purpose formation invoke the nonidentity of such matter.[10] It therefore opens a crack through which a once rejected possibility can be accessed. Matter no longer exists *to serve* us; not to add meaning to human lives; not to be objectified into the very construction or continuation of a singular identity,[11] mannerism, relationships, and faith; not to protect nor to improve the current state of humanity. If truth be told, we are surprisingly close to such an existence as we live to deny its reality – as we continue to choose to live on the other side of our sense of crisis. In an attempt to grapple with a crisis particular to Taiwan, the work *Wafer, Bearer, Deep Rain* by the artist dual lololol stutters. As the work title implies, what is caught up in a single image of microchips is not only a precarious national identity or geopolitical interests, but also environmental and labour exploitation. In other words, the semiconductor industry that is deified and recognised through a hybrid of languages concerning economic growth, political and ecological crisis – and complex emotions such as pride, fear, rage and sense of inadequacy to name a few – is an entangled mass of matter that is assigned with mythical and tragic meaning for the construction of a singular identity. Seemingly distorted and unarticulated, the moving images that appear illusional and unfathomable are grounded in a landscape of the real – things that manifest the industry (an idea) – and change, whilst constituting the island (a physical subject). Formless yet alluring, the work demonstrates the will to re-create what has always been concealed by the disfigurement of the powerful conceptualisations of the Taiwanese semiconductor industry under the dualistic notion of crisis.[12] One finds herself faced directly with the absential, the *non-identity* of a microchip, the semiconductor industry, and if she is willing to admit, Taiwan. Every image in the work stutters to be communicative on the other side of our senses. Perhaps stuttering *is* a language, their language, and *our* language. To begin to explore the other side – all sides – of our senses, we shall begin to stutter. In stuttering, matter does not ask "Do you see me?" from its untameable nature but instead invites us to think *curiously* with their absences.

[1] The Babylonian numeral system is sexagesimal, and both of the numbers 1 and 60 were indicated in a single wedge before the representation of zero came into being. For the history of zero, see Seife, *Zero*.

[2] According to Terrence Deacon, the term "absential" is an "explanation of the emergent and dynamic character of the processes generating living and mental phenomena, rather than the metaphysical paradigm of absentialism." It is "the paradoxical intrinsic property of existing with respect to something missing, separate, and possibly non-existent" (Deacon, *Incomplete Nature*, 577)

[3] Bio art is an art practice in which biology, cells, wet tissues, or parts of living organisms are involved via a scientific or pseudoscientific process of art making.

[4] This visual strategy became a fashion in the art and exhibition making following the development of TV programmes – the ones that mixed documentations of reality with personal accounts from the members involved in the situations – broadcasted through mass media in the west. Such reality could be fictional or staged performances that re-enact past events, e.g., reality shows or investigative documentaries on notorious criminal cases. Bertolt Brecht once commented on the digital production of images, "The situation is becoming so complex that less than ever does a simple reproduction of reality tell us anything about reality."

[5] According to the artist, the in-vitro neural network is not an artificial nor a natural intelligence, therefore its being falls into a "taxonomic void." This should not be confused with the "absential void" that exists outside of any given dualism based on knowledge.

[6] "...object do not go into their concept without leaving a reminder, that they come to contradict the traditional norm of adequacy." (Adorno, *Nagative Dialectics*, p5)

[7] Ibid, p14.

[8] Ibid.

[9] Ibid, p.15, 189.

[10] In Adorno's critique on concept and its material idealism, the truth of all concepts, he says, "refer to nonconceptuality, because concepts on their part are moments of the reality that requires their formation, primarily for the control of nature," and "to change this direction of conceptuality, to give it a turn toward nonidentity, is the hinge of negative dialectics." (Adorno, *Nagative Dialectics*, p11,12)

[11] A singular identity can refer to a personal identity, a national identity or a collective identity in which its formation through assimilation and identification oppresses differences and diversity.

[12] It is not difficult to observe that in the mainstream Taiwanese public discourse, crisis is a concept-reality caught up in the construction of a national identity. In such discourse, absence about, in, of crisis are to be pinned down, conceptualised, replaced and covered for a singularity, e.g., during the global pandemic, the absence of Taiwan in WHO to be defined with the slogan "Taiwan Can Help", narrated and fulfilled through a series of political and material exercises.

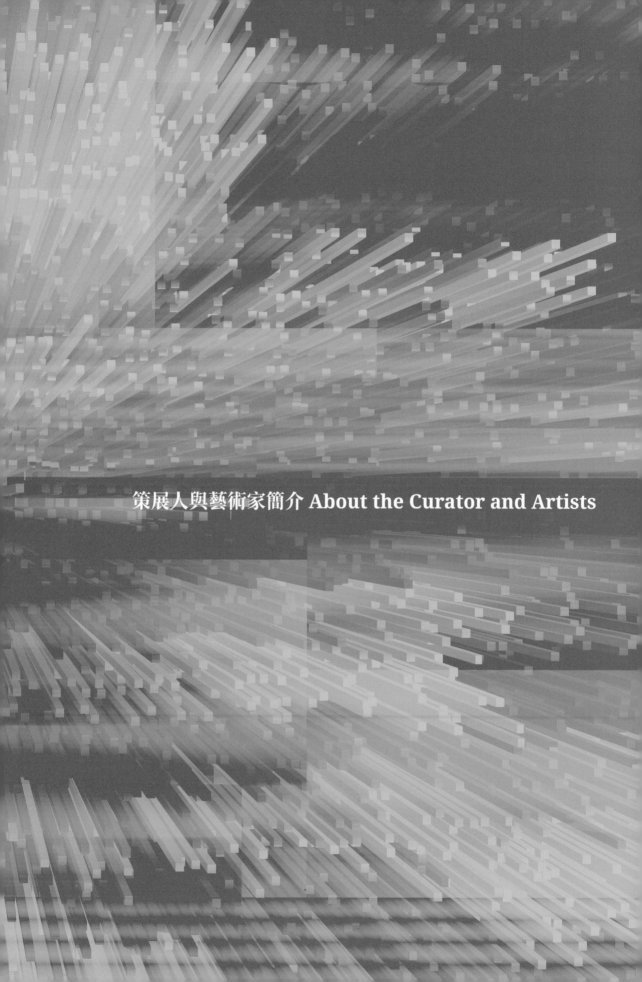

策展人與藝術家簡介 About the Curator and Artists

策展人 ● 孫以臻
CURATOR
● YI-CHENG SUN

1990 年生於臺北臺灣，獨立策展人、社群經營者。近期的關注包括實驗性策展、跨領域協作方法及藝術家老師。她先後畢業於國立臺灣大學生命科學系，及國立臺北藝術大學藝術跨域研究所主修文化生產與策展，目前就讀於國立陽明交通大學科技與社會研究所。雖然曾立志成為探索生命的科學家，但因爲有感於思考及學習受制於學科分類而走向當代藝術策展，自此藝術成為她探索如何生產另類知識的方法。此外，自 2016 年發起「一群人的自學」策展自學社群，並與夥伴每月持續舉辦策展自學聚會後，如何教與如何學也成為她關注並實踐另類知識生產的方法。

Born 1990 in Taipei, Taiwan, Yi-Cheng Sun is an independent curator and a community contributor. Her recent focus includes experimental curating, methods of interdisciplinary co-creation, and teaching-artist. Sun graduated from the Department of Life Science, National Taiwan University, followed by the Graduate Institute of Trans-disciplinary Art at the National Taipei University of Arts, with a concentration in cultural production and curating. She is currently pursuing another degree at the Institute of Science, Technology and Society, National Yang Ming Chiao Tung University. Once aspired to become a scientist exploring what life is, Sun transitioned into contemporary art curating to break away from the limitations that disciplines tends to have over ways of thinking and learning. Art has since become her methodology for exploring the production of alternative knowledge. In 2016, she initiated "Selves-Educating on Curating", a self-learning community for curating, and through organizing monthly member gatherings focusing on self-directed learning of curating, ways to teach and also to learn have also become methods used by Sun in her practice of alternative knowledge production.

藝術家 ● 好奇機 CURIOSKI │ 李懿澔＆鄭伊婷
ARTIST
● CURIOSKI │ YI-HO LI & YI-TING CHENG

好奇機 CURIOSKI 為新媒體藝術團隊，由李懿澔和鄭伊婷兩位藝術家組成，他們以 VR 作為探索心中世界的媒介，實驗影像視覺與身體感受間相互碰撞的可能性。CURIOSKI 認為 VR 不僅只是帶來視覺層面的刺激，而是能將自身對世界之洞察，融入獨特的虛擬裝置體驗中──VR 已成為窺視世界一角的道具，人類終將蛻變成擁有新感官的觀察者。

李懿澔與鄭伊婷，兩位皆畢業於實踐大學媒體傳達設計學系，在學期間一同赴波蘭波茲南藝術大學研修，後分別於 2021 年、2022 年在台灣數位藝術中心舉辦個展。

CURIOSKI is a new media art collective formed by artists Yi-Ho Li and Yi-Ting Cheng. Using virtual reality (VR) as a medium for exploring their inner worlds, they experiment with the interactions between visual images and physical perceptions. CURIOSKI sees VR beyond just visual stimulation but as something that allows their observations of the world to be incorporated into unique virtual installations. VR has become a tool for catching glimpses of the world, and humans are bound to ultimately transform into spectators who are in possession of new senses.

Yi-Ho Li and Yi-Ting Cheng graduated from the Department of Communications Design at Shih Chien University, and they also both studied abroad at the University of the Arts Poznan in Poland. Respectively in 2021 and 2022, their solo exhibitions were presented at the Digital Art Center, Taiwan.

藝術家 ● 黃鼎云
ARTIST
● DING-YUN HUANG

黃鼎云是一位藝術家、劇場編導、戲劇構作,同時也是藝術團體「明日和合製作所」共同創作者。他專注於共同創作、空間回應與跨領域的實踐,也擅長調動觀眾與表演者間的觀演關係。近期發起系列計畫《神的棲所 GiR》、《操演瘋狂》等關注心智、意識與其延伸等相關議題。

作品多發表於亞太地區,亦曾受邀於布魯塞爾藝術節(Kunstenfestivaldesarts)、 柏林高爾基劇院秋天沙龍(Gorki Theater Herbstsalon)、臺北表演藝術中心亞當計畫(ADAM)、皇家墨爾本理工大學(RMIT)、新加坡 Dance Nucleus 等擔任駐節(村)藝術家、協作者、協同策展人。

Ding-Yun Huang is one of the co-founders of Taipei-based multi-creator collective, Co-Coism. He focuses on work-in-collective, site-responding, interdisciplinary practices and skilled at creating a flexible relationship between the audience and the performers. Recently, Ding-Yun initiated a series of projects on "Mind and Consciousness" in the progress of *God in Residency, Performing Insanity*.

His works were mainly premiered in the Asia-Pacific region. He was also invited as a residency artist, facilitator, and guest curator in Kunstenfestivaldesarts (Belgium), Gorki Theater Herbstsalon (Berlin), ADAM—Asia Discover Asia Meetings (Taipei), Royal Melbourne Institute of Technology (Melbourne), Dance Nucleus (Singapore).

藝術家 ● 蓋伊‧班‧阿里
ARTIST
● GUY BEN-ARY

蓋伊‧班‧阿里是一位駐澳洲珀斯的藝術家和研究者。目前在西澳大利亞大學的 SymbioticA 工作,這是一個致力於研究、學習和實踐生命科學的藝術實驗室。班‧阿里跨科學與媒體藝術的藝術實踐橫跨各國,他致力於涉及生物科技的藝術創作,旨在豐富人們對生命意義的理解。作品曾在世界各地著名的館舍與藝術家展出,如北京國立美術館、聖保羅雙年展、莫斯科雙年展等,並受紐約現代美術館永久典藏。他的作品《Bricolage》榮獲日本文化廳媒體藝術祭優勝獎,《cellF》及《Silent Barrage》榮獲林茲電子藝術節榮譽獎(2017,2009),後者也獲得藝術與人造生命範疇的重要獎項 VIDA 一等獎。出自於引起公眾對於介在臨界狀態的生命進行討論的興趣,班‧阿里透過藝術創作,試著問題化新興技術是如何移轉了對於生、死與感知的治理及控制。

Guy Ben-Ary, is a Perth based artist and researcher. He currently works at SymbioticA, an artistic laboratory dedicated to research, learning and hands-on engagement with the life sciences, which is located within the University of Western Australia. Recognized internationally as a major artist and innovator working across science and media arts, Guy specializes in biotechnological artwork, which aims to enrich our understanding of what it means to be alive. Guy's work has been shown across the globe at prestigious venues and festivals from the Beijing National Art Museum to San Paulo Biennale to the Moscow Biennale. His work can also be seen in the permanent collection of the Museum of Modern Art in New York. His work *Bricolage* won an award of excellence in the Japan Media Arts Festival, *cellF* and *Silent Barrage* were awarded Honorary Mentions in Prix Ars Electronica (2017, 2009) and *Silent Barrage* also won first prize at VIDA, a significant international competition for Art and Artificial Life. Interested in how art has the potential to initiate public debate on the challenges arising from the existence of these liminal lives, Guy creates artworks designed to problematize current and emergent bio-technologies' influence on the shifting forces that govern and determine life, death and sentience.

藝術家 ● 胥貝拉・佩區克
ARTIST
● ŠPELA PETRIČ

胥貝拉・佩區克是一位擁有自然科學背景的斯洛維尼亞籍新媒體藝術家。她的藝術實踐結合了表演性以及對生物媒材的實驗，藉此在身體與身體之間建立起奇異的關係，並揭示我們身處的（生物）技術社會的基礎，同時她也試著對此提出替代方案。佩區克曾獲得多項大獎，包括 White Aphroid 的傑出藝術成就獎（斯洛維尼亞）、生物藝術和設計獎（荷蘭）以及林茲電子藝術大獎中的傑出獎（奧地利）。

Špela Petrič is a Slovenian new media artist with a background in the natural sciences. Her artistic practice combines bio-media practices and performativity to enact strange relations between bodies that reveal the underpinnings of our (bio) technological societies and propose alternatives. Petrič has received several awards, such as the White Aphroid for outstanding artistic achievement (Slovenia), the Bioart and Design Award (Netherlands), and an Award of Distinction at Prix Ars Electronica (Austria).

藝術家 ● 動態自造實驗室
ARTIST
● FABLAB DYNAMIC

動態自造實驗室於2013年創立，以「社會設計」為核心方向，透過數位製造技術，針對社會需求而提出持續改善的創新專案，並發展在地特色。藉由跨領域合作，建立跨文化、藝術、設計、工業、建築、製造、環境等多元平臺，鼓勵在製造過程中以開放設計概念，發展「國際化」架構中的「在地化」，達到和國際接軌、創新研發製造等目標。

FabLab Dynamic was founded in 2013. Centering on "social design," the lab utilizes technologies from digital manufacture, and proposes innovative projects targeting different social needs to offer consistent improvement and develop local characteristics. Through interdisciplinary collaboration, the lab strives to establish a diverse platform for interculturality, art, design, industry, architecture, manufacture, and the environment. The lab encourages the concept of open design throughout the production process to facilitate "localization" in "international" frameworks to achieve the objectives of connecting with the global network, innovative research and development, and manufacture.

藝術家 ● lololol｜林亭君 & 張欣
ARTIST ● lololol｜XIA LIN & SHERYL CHEUNG

lololol 是循環的笑聲，0 與 1 構成無盡陰陽變化，同時演示電腦語言的基礎脈動。lololol 時而喜出望外、暗自竊喜或喜怒不形於色；時而發出滄海一聲笑，悠遊在虛實之間的地平線上，不囿於制定的文化邏輯或角色扮演。由藝術家林亭君（臺灣）和張欣（加拿大）於 2013 年共同發起，作為藝術團體主要關心科技生活中的身體政治，借鏡道家思想相關科技論去重新思考我們所身處的世界秩序。

lololol is a cycle of laughter, with endless variables composed with 0's and 1's; at the same time, it is also the fundamental pulse of the computer language. Sometimes joyfully elated, quietly smirking, or emotionally stoic, lololol is also at times a loud enlightened laugh, and sailing on the horizons of virtuality and reality, it is unbounded by conventional cultural logic or role-playing. An art collective co-initiated by artists Xia Lin (Taiwan) and Sheryl Cheung (Canada) in 2013, lololol focuses on body politics in the technology era and references Taoist philosophy to reflect on theories of technology and to reconsider our current world order.

圖錄 Plates

好奇機 CURIOSKI（李懿澕＆鄭伊婷）
CURIOSKI（YI-HO LI & YI-TING CHENG）

《意識景觀系列》
A Glimpse of the Mind Landscapes

《意識景觀系列》由三件 VR 互動裝置構成，探討 VR 科技如何理解從心智哲學出發的意識思考。觀眾將戴上不同的「人腦外掛」，進入三個不同層次的意識景觀，體驗在虛擬情境中的身體經驗如何透過視知覺重新形塑現實世界對於自我及人體存在的解讀。

〈新生〉：外掛一號描繪了一個空白的洞穴世界，觀眾將雙腳浸入水池，讓魚群穿梭於雙腳之間並啄食肉體。此設計試圖讓觀眾覺察自己在虛擬環境中產生的互動行為，能塑造具有現實反饋的體感認知。

〈變異〉：外掛二號中觀眾將脫離人類身型的設定，交付原有的自我意識予另一位虛擬人物，並穿戴上由實驗室提供的新身體，藉由切換視角來實現靈魂轉移，探索自我意識與肉身軀殼的存在關係。

〈出體〉：外掛三號為最高級別的意識景觀。作品中人類意識將能夠脫離「身體載具」的限制，用純粹的意識旅行於不同維度之間。觀眾將穿梭於各種象徵生命的物件，體驗從微觀展開至宏觀的視野。

A Glimpse of the Mind Landscapes is a series composed of three VR interactive installations, and it explores how VR technology comprehends conscious thoughts that have stemmed from the philosophy of mind and cognition. Members of the audience are asked to put on various "external human brains" and enter into three different levels of mind landscapes. The audience will undergo the bodily experience in a virtual realm and understand how the physical world reshapes the interpretation of oneself and physical presence through visual perception.

Plugin01_Rejuvenation: Plugin01 presents an empty cavernous world; the members of the audience are invited to soak their feet in a pool of water, where fish are swimming between their feet and pecking at them. This design attempts to make the audience perceive their interactive behavior in the virtual environment, forming a somatosensory perception that features feedback from reality.

Plugin02_Transformation: Through *Plugin02*, members of the audience could leave their human form, transfer their self-consciousness into another virtual figure, and put on a new body provided by the lab. Soul swapping unfolds here with visual perspectives switched, and thoughts are explored on the existing relationship between one's self-awareness and the corporeal body.

Plugin03_Out-of-body: Plugin03 is the highest level mind landscape. Humans are able to detach their minds from their limiting "corporeal carriers" and embark on a pure voyage of the mind across different dimensions. Members of the audience will be able to shuttle between various objects that symbolize life and engage in an experience that extends from the microscopic to the macroscopic scale.

入口形象區／Entrance Hall
VR 虛擬實境、空間裝置｜10 至 15 分鐘｜尺寸依場地而定｜2022 年
VR, installation｜10-15min.｜Dimensions variable｜2022

黃鼎云
DING-YUN HUANG

《神的棲所 GiR：空耳乩》
God in Residency - Misheard Medium

《神的棲所 GiR：空耳乩》是此計畫的一份階段性紀錄。透過紀錄影像的方式，黃鼎云回到以戲劇導演身分與演員廖原慶展開一場「飾演乩童起乩」的密集排練。兩人從演員的動作與動機分析、內心與情境的摹寫、空間敘事邏輯到表演者與觀者如何共同參演的觀演過程，對於扮演「乩童起乩」之可能的表演技術與方法進行了一連串縝密討論。藉此拆解出日常生活中對宗教信仰的理解方式，也折射出自身實踐與再現之間的兩難——當那個名為「神」的角色進到演員的身體時，難以跨越的或許不是引逗他者神聖經驗之見證，而是演員自身對信仰認知的極限。

God in Residency - Misheard Medium is an on-going documentary of the project's interim progress. The documentary begins with Ding-Yun Huang, who is revisiting his role as a theater director, conducting intensive rehearsals with actor, Yuan-Ching Liao, for the performance of "a medium being possessed by a deity". The two engage in a series of detailed discussions on the possible acting techniques and methods for portraying a medium that is being possessed, including analyses on the actor's movements and motive, portrayals of feelings and scenarios, the logic behind the narrative space, and the audience and performer relationship which involves both parties' collective participation in the performance. Through deconstructing how religion and faith are comprehended in everyday life, the conundrum between personal practice and representation is also reflected: When the character, or the so-called "deity", enters the body of the actor, rather than appealing to others to give testaments on sacred experiences, the hurdle that is difficult to overcome is perhaps how far the actor can push his own faith.

105 展間／R105

單頻道錄像｜15 分 36 秒｜2021 年
Single-channel video｜15 min. 36 sec.｜2021

● 本計畫受臺灣當代文化實驗場 C-LAB「2020 CREATORS LAB」支持
● This project is supported by Taiwan Contemporary Culture Lab (C-LAB)'s "2020 CREATORS LAB".

黃鼎云
DING-YUN HUANG

《神的棲所 GiR：化景練習》
God in Residency - Scenario Incarnation

《神的棲所 GiR：化景練習》探問當非視覺受器受到刺激時，人心中會浮現什麼「影像」？藝術家試圖透過乩童坐禁場景研究與再現，邀請觀眾於展場內實際練習「化景」。宗教性感受是否能夠進一步透過特定機制、環境創造？當觀眾自主進到展間中，閉上眼睛，透過聲音引導展開「與神溝通」的練習。「化景」是坐禁時乩童獲得之能力，在神的旨意下能夠「看見」非物質性的存有與畫面，進而預言、推斷並給予問事者忠告與建議。透過對聲音與視覺之間的關係進行嘗試，《神的棲所 GiR：化景練習》試圖在生理機制上思考「化景」的可能原理。

God in Residency - Scenario Incarnation explores what sort of "images" people may internally conjure when their non-visual receptor is stimulated? The artist studies and recreates the setting of a medium who is undergoing meditative training and invites the audience to practice "scenario incarnation". Can religious experiences be further extended through specific mechanisms and settings? When members of the audience choose to enter into the exhibition space, they are asked to close their eyes, and an audio guide then takes them through practicing "communication with the divine". "Scenario incarnation" is an ability that a medium may acquire through meditative training, which in the will of the deity, they are able to "see" non-material existences and images. The medium is then able to make prophecies, predictions, and give advice and suggestions to the inquirers. Experimenting with the relationship between sound and sight, *God in Residency - Scenario Incarnation* seeks to examine the possible principle behind "scenario incarnation" within the parameters of physiological mechanism.

105 展間／R105
互動裝置、數位輸出│尺寸依場地而定│2022 年
Interactive installation, digital printing│Dimensions variable│2022

找到舒服的位置、閉上眼睛
靜待景物幻化於你
Find a comfortable spot and close your eyes.
Wait for the incarnate scenario occurring to you.

蓋伊・班・阿里
GUY BEN-ARY

《cellF》
cellF

《cellF》是藝術家班‧阿里自畫像式的作品，也是世界上第一件神經聲音合成器。透過在培養皿上的生長，《cellF》的「大腦」由班‧阿里的神經細胞所組成，並且它實時控制著一系列訂製的聲音合成器，是一組全自動的濕式（wet）類比儀器。

班‧阿里從自己的手臂上以活體採檢的方式取得皮膚細胞，並在西澳大學 SymbioticA 的實驗室中進行體外培養，運用誘導多功能幹細胞（iPSC）技術，皮膚細胞被培養為幹細胞。直到這些幹細胞完全分化為神經細胞與網絡後，便與培養皿上的多電極陣列（MEA）相連成「班‧阿里的外部大腦」。

由 8×8 的電極網格組成的多電極陣列承載著神經網絡，這些電極網格可以記錄神經細胞產生的電訊號（動作電位），同時向神經細胞推送電訊號刺激——本質上即為「大腦」讀寫訊息的介面。

神經網絡和類比合成器的工作方式有著驚人的相似之處，兩者都透過傳遞電壓產生數據或聲音。《cellF》並置了這兩者來創建一個相連的新網絡，在音樂家受邀與《cellF》的共演中，人造的音樂作為刺激被傳遞至神經細胞，而神經細胞則透過控制類比合成器做出反應，與音樂家在現場共演著即興且具反射性的後人類音樂篇章。在演出中，這些聲音被空間化到十六個喇叭，並受控於神經網絡以及培養皿中特殊的活動區域。這使得在表演空間中漫步，就如同即時的穿梭在班‧阿里的外部大腦中。

2015 年《cellF》的全球首演與東京的實驗爵士鼓手達倫‧摩爾（Darren Moore）進行了一場獨特的即興表演。達倫‧摩爾的音樂作為電訊號刺激被輸入神經細胞，神經細胞則透過控制合成器創造出即興的後人類音樂篇章。

既不基於人工智能也不基於自然智能的《cellF》處在分類的空白處。在缺乏術語能夠充分解釋其自主性和可塑性的情況下，最好將它理解為擁有「體外智能」的實體：一個借助生物工程所產生，並且在體外如大腦般運作的智能系統（它代表著一種非常早期的體外智能，因而具有某種象徵意義）。《cellF》作為一種體外智能驅動著表演的替代者，它以能夠製造音樂並且進行共同演奏的能耐，替代了細胞捐贈者（班‧阿里）及表演者。

戶外廣場、一樓中樓梯／Plaza & Central Stairway 1F
紀錄片、演出紀錄（影像，2015 年於珀斯、2016 年於雪梨）│6 分 35 秒、4 分 28 秒、8 分 40 秒
演出紀錄（聲音，2017 年於柏林、2017 年於柏林）│43 分 18 秒、33 分 15 秒│2015-2022 年
Documentary film, performance record (video ; 2015 in Perth ; 2016 in Sydney) │
6 min. 35 sec., 4 min. 28 sec., 8min. 40 sec.
Performance record (audio ; 2017 in Berlin ; 2017 in Berlin) │43 min. 18 sec., 33 min. 15 sec. │2015-2022

《cellF》出自藝術家蓋伊‧班‧阿里、內森‧湯普森、達倫‧摩爾以及安德魯‧菲奇的合作；該計畫由西澳大學生物藝術卓越中心 SymbioticA 主辦，並受澳洲政府澳洲藝術理事會協助；資金贊助及諮詢建議則由西澳政府「地方政府、體育和文化產業部門」所提供。
cellF is a collaboration between Guy Ben-Ary, Nathan Thompson, Darren Moore and Andrew Fitch. The project is hosted by SymbioticA, the centre for excellence in Biological Arts at the University of Western Australia. This project has been assisted by the Australian Government through the Australia Council, its arts funding and advisory body and funding provided by the Department of Local Government, Sport and Cultural Industries, Western Australia.

cellF is Guy Ben-Ary's self-portrait but also the world's first neural synthesizer. *cellF*'s "brain" is made of a Ben-Ary's biological neural network that grows in a Petri dish and controls in real-time an array of analogue modular synthesizers that were custom-made to work in synergy with the neural network. It is a completely autonomous, wet and analogue instrument.

Guy Ben-Ary had a biopsy taken from his arm, then he cultivated his skin cells in vitro in the labs of SymbioticA at UWA, and using Induced Pluripotent Stem Cell technology, he transformed his skin cells into stem cells. When these stem cells began to differentiate they were pushed down the neuronal lineage until they became neural stem cells, which were then fully differentiated into neural networks over a Multi-Electrode Array (MEA) dish to become - "Ben-Ary's external brain".

The MEA dishes that host Ben-Ary's neural networks consist of a grid of 8×8 electrodes. These electrodes can record the electric signals (action potentials) that the neurons produce and at the same time send stimulations to the neurons - essentially a read-and-write interface to the "brain".

There is a surprising similarity in the way neural networks and analogue synthesizers work. In both voltages are passed through components to produce data or sound. *cellF*'s neural interface juxtaposes these two networks to create a continuum between the networks. With *cellF*, the musician and musical instrument become one entity to create a cybernetic musician. Human musicians are invited to play with *cellF* in special one-off shows. The human-made music is fed to the neurons as stimulation and the neurons respond by controlling the analogue synthesizers, and together they perform live, reflexive and improvised post-human sound pieces. The sound is spatialized in the space into 16 speakers. The spacialization is controlled by the neural network and reflects the special pockets of activity within the petri dish. Walking around the performance space offers the sensation of walking through Ben-Ary's external brain in real-time.

In its world premiere *cellF* jammed live with Darren Moore, Tokyo-based experimental jazz drummer, in a unique improvisation. His music was fed into the neurons as electrical stimulations and the neurons responded by controlling the synthesizer, creating an improvised post-human sound piece.

Based on neither artificial intelligence nor natural intelligence, *cellF* falls within a taxonomic void. In the absence of terminology that adequately accounts for *cellF*'s autonomy and plasticity, *cellF* is best understood as an entity possessing "in-vitro intelligence": an intelligent system produced by bioengineered living neural networks that function as brains outside of the body (yet it still represents a very early form of in-vitro intelligence, symbolic in a way). *cellF* is an in-vitro intelligence driven surrogate performer; surrogate to its donor (Ben-Ary) and performer for its capacity to make music and duet with a human musician.

胥貝拉・佩區克
ŠPELA PETRIČ

《PL'AI》
PL'AI

《PL'AI》是胥貝拉・佩區克的系列作品《植物機器》當中的第三部，它將「遊戲」的概念視為所有生命體（包括植物）的本體狀態。在《PL'AI》的概念中，遊戲不同於受明確規則或目標限制的賽局，遊戲的行為反映了生命體對存在的好奇心，因此它之於自我認識有著關鍵意義。

在《PL'AI》進行的數個月當中，小黃瓜植株自萌芽便不斷地遊戲，一組人工智慧機器人完全以它為中心進行運算，兩者間的交互作用是彼此「生命中」全部的感知經驗。這場遊戲以超越人類尺度的時間被記錄與運算，預示了一種由植物所形塑的人工智慧，以及相反的，一種受人工智慧干擾所留下的植物型態。

PL'AI, the third work from Špela Petrič's opus *PLANT-MACHINE*, embraces the notion of a play as an ontological condition of all living bodies, including plants. The act of playing, unlike games, which are limited by clear rules or goals, reflects the curiosity of existence and is therefore at the heart of (self) knowing.

PL'AI is a process lasting several months in which cucumber plants were grown from seed and an AI-robot whose perceptual world is limited to them, interacts with each other. The play beyond the human time scale promises a glimpse of artificial intelligence as formed by the plant and, conversely, a morphology of the plant imprinted by the interventions of the robot.

106 展間／R106

AI 裝置、機器人、小黃瓜植株、金屬框、電腦與支架、雷射光與攝影機臺車、鋼繩與彩色球體、攝影機｜2020 年
AI based installation, robot, live cucumber plants, metal frame, racks with computers, LiDAR trolley with camera, steel wires with color balls, cameras｜2020

● 本作展出形式由原 AI 裝置作品，轉製為紀錄片與雙頻道錄像。
紀錄片，12 分 18 秒，2020 年｜雙頻道錄像，10 分，2022 年
● The exhibition format of this work has been transformed from the original AI based installation work into a documentary and dual-channel video.
Documentary film, 12 min. 18 sec, 2020｜Two-channel video, 10 min., 2022

Credits:
程式設計 Programming: Benjamin Fele, Tim Oblak
機器人開發 Robot development and assembly: Gregor Krpič, Erik Krkač, Jože Zajc, David Pilipovič
設計 Design: Miha Turšič
特別感謝 Thanks to: Adriana Knouf, Agnieszka Wolodzko
製作 Produced by: Kersnikova Institute, Kapelica Gallery within the framework of the European ARTificial Intelligence Lab
共同贊助 Co-funded by: Creative Europe Programme of the European Union, Ministry of Culture of the Republic of Slovenia, Ministry of Public Administration of the Republic of Slovenia, City of Ljubljana - Department of Culture, Creative Industries Fund NL, and Dutch Science Foundation NWO, Smart Hybrid Forms grant
製作合作 Produced in cooperation with: ZKM | Karlsruhe, MU Hybrid Art House, VU Artscience laboratory hybrid forms

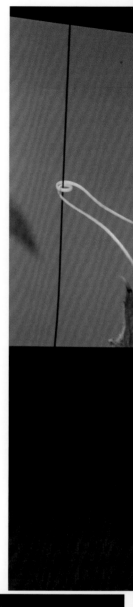

動態自造實驗室
FABLAB DYNAMIC

《Project ZERO｜首部曲》
Project ZERO｜Episode One

在面對無法避免的身體消逝之後，有可能透過日新月異的科技，來延續個人的思維嗎？而科技的進步，又能否在生命終點之後，承襲個人的精神意志和思考脈絡，繼而從中生長出新的創作，成為新生的後盾？在這因時間斷點所切割而生的未知領域中，《Project ZERO｜首部曲》試圖超越時空的跨距，從已故傳奇舞者蕭賀文出發，以去脈絡化的影像、數據為主體的敘述文本，探究生命消亡與科技發展之間的關係，並期待與嘗試在未來，能以姿態辨識、人工智慧、演算法等技術發展，產生新的意識與思考。《Project ZERO｜首部曲》邀請觀者踏上一段搜尋數位足跡的旅程，拼湊出舞者的生命歷程和創作軌跡，共同參與一場具有實驗性質的感知體驗。

Facing the inevitable disappearance of the physical body, would it be possible to continue an individual's mind through rapidly advancing technology? Would technological advancement be able to, after the end of one's life, inherit the person's spirit, will, and thinking to further create new works and support this new existence? In this unknown realm produced by the stopping point of life, *Project ZERO｜Episode One* attempts to transcend time and space, and uses a narrative text comprising decontextualized images and data based on the dearly departed dance legend, Hsiao Ho-Wen, to explore the connections between the disappearance of life and technological development, while hoping and trying to generate new consciousness and thinking in the future through the technological developments related to posture recognition, artificial intelligence, and algorithm. *Project ZERO｜Episode One* invites the audience to embark on a search for digital footprints to piece together the dancer's life journey and creative trajectories, participating collectively in an experimental experience of sensory perception.

107 展間／R107
VR 虛擬實境｜10 分｜2021 年
VR｜10 min.｜2021

● 本計畫受 2021 年高雄電影節原創 VR 單元支持
● This project is supported by 2021 Kaohsiung Film Festival, Kaohsiung VR Film Lab Originals.

在面對無法避免的身體消逝之後，是否可能透過日新月異的科技

延續個人的思考脈絡？而科技的進步，又帶著生命觀點之後，利

個人的精神意志，藉兩控中生長出新的創作，成為新生的依賴？在

因時間斷點所切割出的未知領域中，《Project Zero》首部曲以嶄新

時空的跨距，從已故藝者養裏實文出發，以去重啟此的影像、靈

為主體的敘述文本，探究生命消亡與科技發展之間的關係。

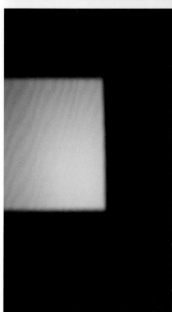

lololol（林亭君 & 張欣）
lololol（XIA LIN & SHERYL CHEUNG）

《晶舟靈雨》
Wafer Bearer Deep Rain

半導體是建設未來的必要基礎設施，在持續「調變」的世界經脈中，臺灣作為半導體產業的聚集地，是全球科技生產的縮影，技術物在此製造、損耗、消亡與重生，皆與人們的生活發生著千絲萬縷的聯繫。延續 lololol 藝術雙人組長期以來對自然、工業、電子環境的迭代觀察與現象回應，藝術家透過自身在城市山水中的生活情境，以多重敘事的錄像聲音裝置，來調節科技物件以及人類之間的能量關係，有機的去想像全球／地方半導體的技術現實。

乘著風雨聲調潮起潮落，你來我往，掀起一陣無形風波。
一葉晶舟在搖搖晃晃的動態平衡中，飄移，流動，互存共生的生存狀態。

Semiconductors are essential infrastructure for building the future, and in this continuously shifting and modulating world, Taiwan, as a semiconductor hub, is an epitome of the global technology production. Technical objects are produced, exhausted, eliminated, and reborn here, and all of which are inextricably linked with people's lives. Extending from the artist duo lololol's long-term iterated observations and responses on the phenomena of natural, industrial, and electronic environments, the collective applies everyday scenarios from their surrounding urban landscapes and uses a multi-narrative audio-visual video installation to regulate the dynamic relationship between technical objects and human beings and to organically imagine the technological reality behind semiconductors on both global and local scales.

Along with the wind and sounds of the rain,
tides get high and fall low,
setting off an invisible storm, as you come and I go.

A wafer bearer sways in dynamic balance,
drifting, floating in symbiotic coexistence.

108 展間／R108
錄像裝置｜尺寸依場地而定｜2022 年
Video installation｜Dimensions variable｜2022

● 此計畫概念於 2021 年與藝術家團體 eteam 合作發起
● The conception of this project started in 2021 with close collaboration with artistic collective eteam.

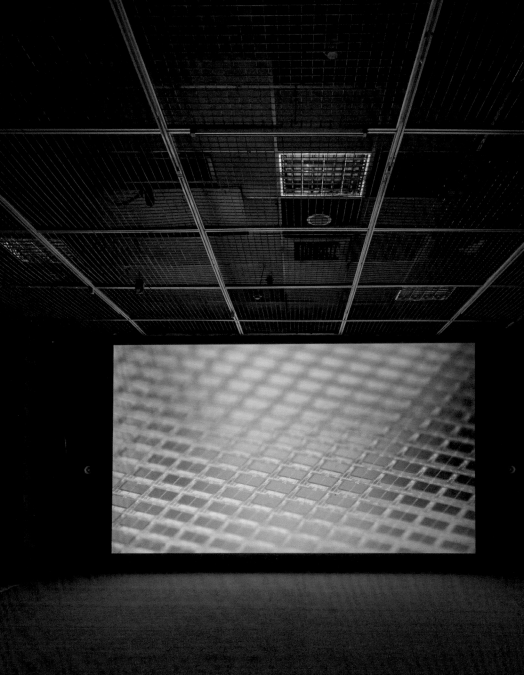

Bearer of shadows boxing with light

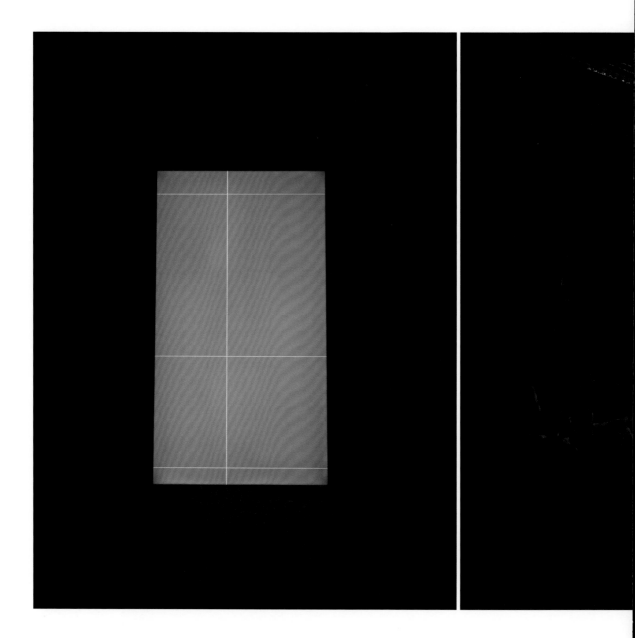

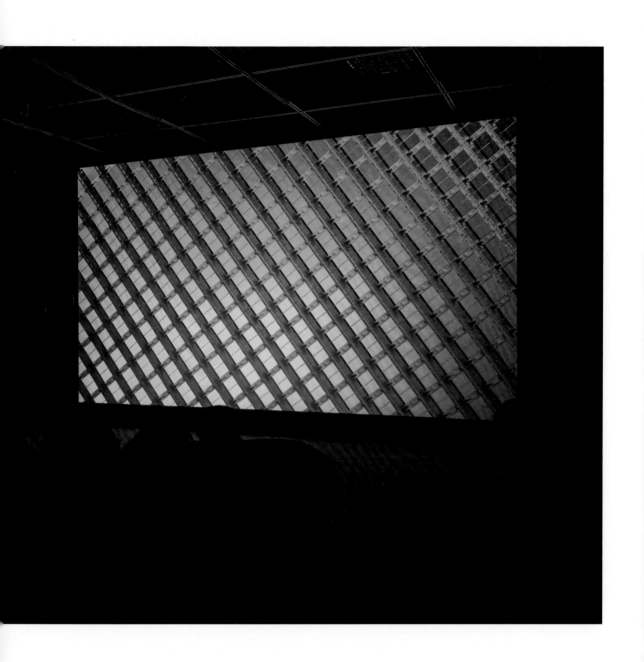

專輯執行

發行者｜財團法人台北市文化基金會
總編輯｜駱麗真
美術編輯｜陳彥如、魏妏如
展場攝影｜王世邦
翻譯｜廖蕙芬、游騰緯、黃亮融、謝雨珊

出版者｜財團法人台北市文化基金會台北當代藝術館
地址｜103 臺北市大同區長安西路 39 號
電話｜+886-2-2552-3721
傳真｜+886-2-2559-3874
網址｜www.mocataipei.org.tw
印刷｜奇異多媒體印藝有限公司
定價｜新臺幣 850 元
初版｜2023 年 12 月
ISBN｜978-626-96983-6-3

本專刊編輯著作權屬於臺北市政府文化局所有
翻印必究 ©

Editorial Team

Publisher: Taipei Culture Foundation
Chief Editor: Li-Chen Loh
Designers: Yanru Chen, Wenru Wei
Photographer: Anpis Wang
Translators: Hui-Fen Anna Liao, Tony Yu,
Liang-jung Huang, Catherine Y. Hsieh

Published by Taipei Culture Foundation / Museum of
Contemporary Art, Taipei
Address: No. 39, Chang-An West Road, Taipei, Taiwan
Telephone: +886-2-2552-3721
Fax: +886-2-2559-3874
Website: www.mocataipei.org.tw
Printed by CHIYI MEDIA PRINTING CO., LTD.
Price: TWD 850
First Published in December, 2023
ISBN: 978-626-96983-6-3

Copyright by the Department of Cultural Affairs, Taipei
City Government, all rights reserved.

指導單位
Supervisor

台北市文化局

主辦單位
Organizers

北 台北市文化基金會
Taipei Culture Foundation

台北當代藝術館
MoCA TAIPEI

贊助單位
Sponsors

THERMOS.

當代藝術基金會
Contemporary Art Foundation

財團法人
紀慧能藝術文化基金會

 royal inn 老爺會館

年度指定投影機
Annual Sponsor for
Appointed Projector

EPSON
EXCEED YOUR VISION

年度指定電視 / 螢幕
Annual Sponsor for
Appointed TV / Screen

SONY

媒體協力
Media Cooperation

Rti 中央廣播電臺
Radio Taiwan International

特別感謝
Special Thanks

台北電影節
TAIPEI FILM FESTIVAL

yogibo
TAIWAN

共識覺：主題樂園幻想工程挑戰賽＝ The proto-ocean for co-
consciousness : making worlds an imagineering project ／駱
麗真總編輯・──初版・──臺北市：財團法人臺北市文化基金會
臺北當代藝術館出版：財團法人臺北市文化基金會發行，2023.12
　　面；　公分
中英對照
ISBN 978-626-96983-6-3（平裝）

1.CST: 數位藝術 2.CST: 數位媒體 3.CST: 作品集

956.7　　　　　　　　　　　　　　　　112021074